Teddy Bear
of
Bumpkin Hollow

By SHARON BOUCHER

Illustrated by DEAN BRYANT

RAND McNALLY & COMPANY · CHICAGO
Established 1856

TEDDY was a little brown bear. He was just about the cutest little brown bear that ever lived in Bumpkin Hollow. But he had one very bad habit. No matter what his mama told him to do—he wanted to do just the opposite.

If Mama Bear said, "Teddy, it's time to come in and eat lunch now," Teddy would stay right where he was and play and play.

If Mama Bear said, "Teddy, it's time to go
to sleep now," he would just open his eyes
as wide as wide and say, "But, Mama, I'm
not sleepy."

No matter what Mama wanted him to do, he didn't want to do it. Why, if Mama told him to be a good boy and smile, he would make the most awful face. It was enough to scare Sammy Squirrel right out of his skin. Even Willie Woodpecker stopped pecking

holes in the White Pine tree and hid his head under his left wing when Teddy made a face like that.

Mama and Papa Bear talked about Teddy's strange behavior one evening after Teddy was asleep.

"What will we do!" Mama Bear said, completely exasperated.

"I am sure I do not know," said Papa. "He is getting too big to spank."

"Spanking doesn't do a bit of good, anyway," said Mama. "Making him stand in the corner doesn't do any good. Putting him to bed in the middle of the day doesn't do any good, either."

"I don't know," said Papa. "I really don't know what to do."

Mama Bear thought a long time. Finally she said, "I know—I know *exactly* what to do."

"What?" asked Papa Bear.

"What does Teddy like to do the very best of anything?" Mama asked him.

"Why, to go across Bumpkin Hollow, up Blue Lupine Hill, down through Bobcat Canyon, and 'way up on Chocolate Mountain to visit Grandma and Grandpa Bear," said Papa.

"Then we shall go to Chocolate Mountain tomorrow morning," Mama said. "But we shall wait and see if Teddy goes or if Teddy stays at home."

"But he can't stay alone," said Papa.

"No, of course not, but Cousin Amanda will be glad to stay with him, I know," said Mama.

Early the next morning Mama called to Teddy, "Hurry, Teddy, the sun is up and it is time for little bears to be up, too."

Teddy didn't even grunt.

Mama called him again, but still he didn't wake up.

Mama had to call him six times because, of course, he didn't want to do anything he was told to do.

After breakfast Mama gave him a shiny red bucket. "Go over to Honey Bee Hive," she said, "and get this bucket full of the very best Mountain Flower Honey.

"Take the short path and not the long one through the Green Woods," she warned. "Now hurry, Teddy. If you are back by ten o'clock, you will have a very pleasant surprise. If you are not back by then, you will be very sorry."

"What is the surprise?" asked Teddy. Teddy just loved surprises.

"I can't tell you now," said Mama, "or it wouldn't be a surprise any longer. Now run along, and remember, *don't go through the woods.*"

Teddy ran down the path swinging the shiny red bucket. Soon he came to the little twisted path that went under the wild grape-vines and into the woods.

Teddy stopped. How he did love to go through the Green Woods and wade in the icy mountain stream!

"Oh, dear," said Teddy. "What shall I do? I wonder what the old surprise is anyway." He stood there swinging his bucket.

"I'll hurry," said Teddy. "I'll run as fast as I can. Then it won't take me any longer to go through the woods than to go by the short path."

And Teddy crawled under the wild grape-vines and scampered down the little twisted path into the Green Woods. Soon he came to the icy mountain stream.

"I'll just take a minute to splash in it," he said to himself. Then he saw Mr. Bull Frog on a rock.

"Good morning," croaked Mr. Frog. "I'm so glad to see you, Teddy Bear. I have been learning a new song. Do sit down and listen, and tell me what you think of it."

Teddy sat down on the cool green bank and wiggled his toes in the icy water.

Mr. Frog croaked his very loudest. "What do you think of that?" he asked when he was through.

"That is fine," said Teddy. "That is a very fine song."

"Let me sing you another," said Mr. Bull
Frog.

"No," said Teddy, suddenly remembering
the surprise, "I must hurry over to Honey
Bee Hive."

So on he went.

Just as Teddy was coming out of the Green Woods, he met Timothy Black Bear. Timothy was also on his way to Honey Bee Hive. Timothy and Teddy raced and played tag all the way up the hill. They were so tired by the time they came to Honey Bee Hive that they sat down on an old pine log to rest . . . .

Soon they were fast asleep. Teddy began to snore. Well, Mr. Honey Bee didn't like that terrible noise going on right under his bee-hive. He flew out in an awful rage and stung Teddy right on the end of his little black nose.

"Here's your honey," he said. "Now go on home." Oh, Mr. Honey Bee was cross.

Teddy snatched up the shiny red bucket of honey and ran howling down the path. He

didn't turn off into the woods this time. He just ran right straight for home as fast as his short little legs would carry him.

He wanted Mama Bear to put some soft black mud on his nose to take the sting away.

But when Teddy got home, Mama Bear wasn't anywhere to be found. Papa Bear wasn't anywhere, either. And there on Mama Bear's favorite chair sat Cousin Amanda.

When Teddy saw her he wailed, "Where's my mama? I want my mama."

"Oh," said Cousin Amanda, "your mama and papa left here at ten o'clock this morning. They went across Bumpkin Hollow, up Blue Lupine Hill, down through Bobcat Canyon, and 'way up on Chocolate Mountain to visit Grandma and Grandpa Bear. You could have gone with them if you had been back on time."

Teddy Bear didn't know what to do. He just stood there for a minute looking very, very sad.

Then he ran over to his little soft bed, buried his head under the pine-needle pillow, and cried and cried and cried.

Late that afternoon Mama Bear and Papa Bear came home. Teddy had been thinking. When he saw Mama Bear, he ran to her.

He put his arms around her. "I won't *ever* be a naughty little bear again," he promised.

"Of course you won't," said Mama Bear. "Look what Grandma Bear sent home for you—big chocolate cookies with white sugar frosting. And she wants you to come and see her next week."

And Teddy went.